THE TALE TRAVELERS

TRAVELERS

BOOK 1

THE TALE TRAVELERS BOOK 1

Henry's History

Reji Laberje

To order additional copies of this book, contact:
Xlibris Corporation
1-888-795-4274
www.Xlibris.com
Orders@Xlibris.com

36573

CONTENTS

DEDICATION

For Lee Braunel, my first and favorite storyteller; if in my telling of tales I manage to touch a fraction of the number of lives touched by you in your teaching of them, I shall call myself successful. Moreover, I shall call myself honored.

Additional special thanks to my two sisters, Kim and Stacy, and more great friends than I can begin to list, without whose support this book wouldn't be here today. Also, to Donald, for making me a better writer; I'm lucky to have worked with you.

CHAPTER 1

To the Library

HENRY, FAY, MICHAEL, and Patty had just moved from Chicago, Illinois, to the small farming town of Valders, Wisconsin. The new house, once a farmhouse, was big and old. It creaked when people opened or closed doors or when they went up and down the stairs. Each of the kids got their own room with a little porch, and the yard was big enough for their chubby black Lab to run laps. None of it mattered though. The Smith siblings were not happy.

Valders had no movie theater, no laser-tag club, no arcade, no mall, and, so far, no fun! They didn't have cable television, and their dad still hadn't set up the computer. As if it could get any worse, the moving company that packed up their old home left behind a box that contained all of their video games. There really was nothing to do.

On nice days, Henry would help his dad in the yard. At first, it was fun. Henry's dad, a principal in Chicago, but soon to be a substitute teacher in Valders, looked older than he was. He had gray hair and wore glasses. He usually looked very tired from working so many hours. Moving to Valders meant that he would get to work fewer hours though, and now Henry would see him more. So every day, the two would clear sticks and rocks, rake, spread grass seeds, and water the lawn that had been neglected for many months. It was nice to spend so much time with his dad, but now he was certain he'd had enough of that to last him the rest of the summer.

Henry was ten years old, and he moped about the new house in baggy jeans and T-shirts with his rarely combed sandy brown hair falling every which way but straight over his fair-skinned, freckled face. He was very angry that he had to leave Chicago. He would be in the fifth grade after this summer, and he wished he could have been at the top of his school with his old friends.

Michael and Patty were eight years old. They were twins and, except for shaggy ponytails on Patty, looked it. They had the same fair skin as their brother Henry, but with only a single freckle each and lighter hair. Michael usually wore buttoned shirts and shorts with his sports socks pulled all the way up to his knees. Patty, being a bit of a tomboy, was usually dressed similarly or in some type of overalls.

Every day since the move, Michael grumbled, "I'm bored."

"Me too," Patty would say.

Then Fay, their seven-year-old sister, would ask, "Why did we have to move?" in a small and whining voice. Usually she brushed her thick curls off of her shoulder as she spoke. Fay was every bit a little princess in floral dresses, matching sandals, and colored barrettes in her long light brown hair. Beneath her little pink lips and cheeks were the same fair skin and freckles brandished by her big brother, Henry.

"There's nothing to do in this stupid place," Henry would always add.

After two weeks of the same complaints, their mom, Mrs. Smith—a young mom with very short brown hair and a dozen activities going on at any given time—asked the neighbor where she could bring her kids to have some fun.

Their neighbor was a pretty older woman. She was always smiling, and she smelled nice. She had the strangest eyes though. She looked more like a child, just like the Smith siblings, when you looked at those huge green eyes. They were surrounded by the biggest, thickest, longest black lashes Patty had ever seen. The outside lashes were so long that it made the woman's eyes look like they were always smiling. Her name was Hope Fable. She told Mrs. Smith all about the town library. It was a small building that had been in Valders for much longer than Hope had even known.

"You ought to bring the kids in tomorrow," said Mrs. Fable. "I'm a storyteller there. It's great fun!"

"A library?" objected Henry. "That sounds boring!"

"Oh no," responded Mrs. Fable, "not this library. This library is unlike any other you've known."

"How do you know?" snapped Henry.

"I just do," Hope smiled warmly at him as she said it.

"Is it big?" Michael asked. "We had a big library in Chicago. It was three floors high. I went there on a school field trip."

"Well, no. It's not really big," she answered while shaking her head.

"Does it have a playroom?" wondered Patty. "Puzzles and stuffed animals and things like that?"

"No," said their new neighbor, "there isn't a playroom."

"No fun!" whined Fay.

"Well, what is there?" snapped Henry.

"Books, of course," said Mrs. Fable.

"I'm too old for story time, anyway. It sounds boring!" mumbled Henry.

"Oh, but it isn't. You come down tomorrow, and I'll show you. It is a very special place. I promise," Mrs. Fable said with a smile.

Mrs. Smith apologized for the way her children spoke to their new neighbor and said she would bring them to the library the next afternoon.

Just as it had every day since they moved, the time passed slowly the next day. When Henry had awakened, he looked out his bedroom window and saw that it was raining. He had been hoping it would be sunny. Then he could work with his dad in the yard instead of going to the library. As tired of it as he was, working outside was still better than a bunch of books.

"Hey, big guy!" said Mr. Smith with a smile when Henry came down the stairs for cereal. "So you're going to the library today?"

"Yeah," groaned Henry.

By the afternoon though, Henry, Michael, Patty, and Fay were *so* bored that even a dull library trip sounded like a good idea. So after lunch, they all piled into the family's van, and Mrs. Smith took them to town.

"This is it?" Fay said when they stopped in front of a small stone building ten minutes later. On the front lawn, there was an old wooden sign that read "Valders Town Library: An Adventure in Every Book!"

"I guess so," said Mrs. Smith. Even she looked a little surprised at the size of the library. It was no bigger than their house, maybe smaller, in fact. She led Henry, Michael, Patty, and Fay inside where Mrs. Fable was happily waiting for them.

"Good afternoon!" Mrs. Fable declared. "I'm so happy that you kiddos made it today! The other children aren't here just yet."

Henry rolled his eyes at the word "kiddos." He was almost in middle school! This was definitely going to stink.

"Hope," asked Mrs. Smith, "would you mind if I went next door to the small grocery store for a few minutes? I just have a couple of things I need to pick up for the house."

"No problem," she answered. "I have a lot to show them. The librarian comes late on storyteller days, so I'm in charge."

"Do you need anything?" Mrs. Smith added kindly.

"No, dear." Hope smiled. "Thanks for asking."

With that, Mrs. Smith left, and the four of them were left standing in the little library staring at the walls. It was a small place, but every inch of space was filled. The books went from the floor to the ceiling with big ladders on wheels that circled the whole room. There was no space for windows or even a painting. There were books of every size—big ones, small ones, some so thick that they came up to Fay's waist when closed and some so tiny that you could put them in the palm of your hand. There were books of every color in the rainbow, plus gold and silver and copper. There were even books of different shapes. Small square ones that looked like building blocks filled tiny holes on the walls. There were triangular books and circular ones and others shaped as hearts and diamonds.

Michael, who loved playing with cars almost as much as reading, ran right up to one book that was shaped like a stop sign. He read aloud, "*Stop! The Many Signs of Our Streets.*" Patty found a book that was shaped like a shoe that even had real laces of bright red and yellow.

Henry spotted a computer on a small desk in the middle of the room. Barely noticing the books filling the library shelves, walls, and tables, he walked over to the computer and started pushing buttons.

"What's wrong with this thing?" he asked Mrs. Fable.

"Nothing, dear," she replied as she walked toward him. "It doesn't have any games. It's a card catalog. It's used to look for books. Here, let me show you."

Mrs. Fable looked over Henry's shoulder and started to show him how to find a book on one of the shelves using the card catalog program on the computer. After a moment though, they heard a call of "Fay, come back here!" Patty was running after Fay. Fay had gone through a small door at the very back of the library, and Patty was right behind her.

"Oh, girls, no!" cried out Mrs. Fable frantically. She ran to the back just as Patty also stepped through the door. "Don't go in there, I said!"

Reaching the small door, Mrs. Fable peeked inside and then turned around to see that Michael and Henry were coming over as well. She very quickly shut the door. Then she stood in front of the small entrance, blocking the way from the two boys.

"I'm afraid it's too late, boys," she said. "They've gone in."

CHAPTER 2

Enter at Your Own Risk

"WHY CAN'T THEY go in there?" Henry demanded to know.

"Well, it's not that they can't." Mrs. Fable began. "It's just that I was hoping to prepare you for . . . *those* books."

"Why?" asked Michael.

"What do you mean by *those* books?" Henry questioned her.

"The books in this room are special," she replied. She pointed to a sign on the door.

WARNING!!!

Books in this room require:

A love of reading,   An active imagination,   And a strong sense
of adventure.

Once you begin a story, you must complete it.

NO EDITING ALLOWED!

ENTER AT YOUR OWN RISK!

"Let us in there!" snapped Henry. He may be only ten years old, he thought, but he was still the oldest Smith kid here; and he wasn't going to let something bad happen to his sisters if he could help it.

Just then, they heard two loud slams.

"Oh my," sighed Mrs. Fable. "I really can't, kiddos." The storyteller bit her lip nervously.

"What was that?" Michael said in a frightened voice. He stepped just slightly behind his big brother.

"The books have closed," she said. "They'll be checked out now." As she said this, she looked very worried, and she put a gentle hand on the door.

"I'm going in," Henry decided aloud. He pushed by Mrs. Fable and into the room behind the door.

"Henry, no!" shouted Michael. He grabbed Henry's shirttail, but it was too late.

"Well, I guess it's just us then, isn't it?" Mrs. Fable looked down at Michael and held out her hand. She took a deep breath and smiled. "We can't let him do it alone now, can we?" she asked.

Cautiously, Michael took the storyteller's hand, and she led him through the door. The two of them joined Henry who was standing in the center of the room looking straight up, like a child at the foot of a very tall skyscraper. Neither he nor Michael spoke a word. Hope stood back and watched the two boys take in the room.

The room was lit by five hanging lanterns with golden orange colored fires glowing inside of them. Each lantern was by one of five single books. But these weren't just any books. They were nothing like what the boys expected. These were the most gigantic books Henry and Michael had ever seen in their entire lives. Each book was as tall as the room and wide enough to drive through. The books looked very old. The thick, beaten covers of the giant objects might have been colored once but now were faded and dusted in a brownish gray film. The leathery books were worn at the corners, which now looked soft and round. In beautiful giant gold writing, Henry read the titles, "*History, Mythology, Pioneer Days, Fairy Tales,* and *Sam's Science.*"

Sam's Science was unlike the other stories. It had a sort of cage around it of large rusty bars. There were chains holding the bars together and an enormous lock with twenty-six different keyholes—each shaped like a different letter of the alphabet. Tied by a string to the lock was a small yellow tag that read "checked out for the duration" in red ink.

"What does that mean?" asked Michael as he read the tag.

Henry gave a small start when Michael broke the silence. He had still been staring around the cavernous room at the strange oversized books.

"Well, until the story is over, of course." Mrs. Fable said to Michael. Her big eyes seemed to hold some deeper meaning.

"This is some kind of trick. I bet the girls just found some back door out of here or . . . or . . . or *something*. They're probably sitting out there right now laughing at us," said Henry. He angrily stormed out of the room to look for Patty and Fay.

Michael was about to follow Henry when he heard a scratching sound from above. He turned toward the sound and looked up. Right before his eyes, he saw extra letters appearing on two of the books. Above *Fairy Tales*, the letters F-A-Y-S came up one at a time as if a large invisible hand were writing them there. Then P-A-T-T-Y-S was spelled above *Pioneer Days* in the same way. The books now read *Fay's Fairy Tales* and *Patty's Pioneer Days*.

"Wow!" exclaimed Michael. He felt scared. At the same time he was very curious. "She's excited," Michael whispered.

"Who's excited?" Mrs. Fable asked.

"Oh, my sister Patty is. It's stupid, I know. But sometimes, I can tell how she feels. My mom says it's because we're twins. I just think it's because she's so bossy and always tells me how she feels!" Michael complained.

"Oh, that's all it is, you think?" prodded the storyteller.

"I don't know. Nobody would believe that other stuff about feeling the same things, would they?" he shrugged back, a little embarrassed.

"I wouldn't say that, Michael," answered Mrs. Fable. "I believe you. You might even say I . . ." Mrs. Fable's voice trailed off for a moment, and then she took a deep breath and smiled down at Michael in a knowing way. "I understand you," she finished with a wink.

"Doesn't matter. Anyway, Patty thinks she can boss me around just because she was born before me. But only by an hour!" Michael snapped.

"You're older than Fay though," Mrs. Fable offered.

"I know. She's not bossy like Patty, but she sure whines a lot," Michael said.

"They're not here now," Mrs. Fable replied. "What would you do if you could make a choice without them?"

Michael thought for a moment.

"You like books, don't you, Michael?" Hope smiled to him.

Michael looked up at the book titled *Mythology* as, slowly, its massive cover began to creak open.

Meanwhile, in the other room, Henry had decided that Fay and Patty must have been hiding in the room with the large books and was ready to give up his search and go back in there yet again. This whole thing was all a big joke on him. It had to be. Just as he turned to go into the small room, the entire building shook with the sound of metal crashing to the ground. Henry fell flat on his butt. He got back up, but as he began to walk again, the same crashing metal sound shook the building again, knocking him backward. Now, he was afraid. He got up and began running to the back room. He heard a loud slam just like the sound he and Michael had first heard before going into the room. He stayed on his feet this time and ran as fast as he could into the small back room.

When he got there, Michael was gone.

Henry looked at the giant books and saw the new titles of *Fay's Fairy Tales* and *Patty's Pioneer Days*. He also noticed that these books had cages around them now, just like *Sam's Science*.

"What have you done with my brother and sisters?" yelled Henry. "Where are they? Tell me. Tell me!"

Mrs. Fable was not nearly as upset as Henry. Instead, she was whistling while she pulled some yellow paper and a red pen from her pocket.

"Answer me!" he screamed. "What's going on?"

Still, Mrs. Fable didn't say a word. She wrote on the small yellow tags and then pulled some string from her other pocket. She walked over to the newly caged books and began tying on the tags on which she had written, "checked out for the duration."

Before Henry could get out another word, he heard a scratching sound and looked up to see the title of one of the mysterious books change before his eyes. It now read *Michael's Mythology*. He stepped toward the book but was stopped as a large metal cage slammed down upon it with such speed that Henry jumped back for fear of being hurt. That was the crashing metal sound he had heard earlier. One by one, Henry watched in stunned silence as links began forming a chain around the bars and a lock with twenty-six keyholes, like those on (now) three of the other books, appeared out of thin air.

Henry stood in amazement for a moment. Mrs. Fable was writing another tag. He took a deep breath to scream because he felt like that was what he should do. Instead of screaming, he began to cough and gasp. He had inhaled a cloud of dust. Where did it come from? Out of the corner of his eye, Henry spotted the source of the dust. The gigantic cover of *History* began to slowly open, brushing against the floor as it did so. The tops of the pages were sprinkling down dust as though it were snow.

Oh no, thought Henry. He didn't know what was going on, but he didn't think he wanted to be a part of it. He tried to go out of the room, but the dust was making him cough so hard that he had fallen to his knees and his eyes were watering. He sneezed to clear the tickle in his nose and throat. He stood to make his escape. Then he felt a ferocious breeze. He turned and saw that the book was now completely open and the pages were turning at a very rapid pace blowing Henry's clothing and hair about. Henry knew he could handle no more of this. Just then . . . the book stopped.

He felt as though it was his heart that had stopped. What was all this? He looked over at Mrs. Fable who was calmly making another yellow tag. She smiled at him. "How do you feel about history, Henry?" she asked with a wink.

"I . . ."

Before he finished answering, a single page grew out of the center of the book, shot straight out from the pages, wrapped around Henry, and rolled up quickly, snapping Henry with it back into the book which slammed shut.

Henry was spinning and spinning. He felt dizzy, and his stomach was turning. Was he going to be sick? He saw hundreds of thousands of words in all different languages flashing before his eyes. Finally, praying that the turning would end soon, he gave up and simply closed his eyes. After what seemed like an eternity, he felt himself slow down enough to cautiously reopen them.

He landed with a thud on the grounds outside of a large stone castle. There were people everywhere, and it was loud, but Henry felt completely lost and alone. He still didn't understand what was happening, but he had a sneaking suspicion that this might just be a part of *Henry's History*.

CHAPTER 3

Enterprise of the Indies

H ENRY LOOKED DOWN at himself. He was now wearing a long red robe, a ruffled shirt, pointed shoes, and red tights! He reached up to scratch his head and felt a velvet hat. Velvet!

"Oh, man! I'm dressed like a girl," he said aloud.

"Not for the year 1492, you aren't," said a kind voice from behind him.

Henry jumped. When he turned, he saw an older woman dressed in brightly colored velvet and lace. At first, he thought she was a stranger, but when he looked closer at the face behind the lace veil and noticed the huge green eyes with those long black eyelashes, he realized it was none other than Mrs. Fable. "Hey!" he shouted, reaching out toward the woman. She didn't even flinch.

"You don't want to do that now, Henry," she said sweetly. "I'm your ally in these pages."

At that moment, Henry noticed that the sound of the crowds around him had gone silent. He turned to look at them, and everybody had frozen. It was as if he had hit the pause button on the world around him.

"I'm not really here with you," said Mrs. Fable. "I'm just a tour guide of sorts."

"A what?" he asked with confusion.

"I am the Narrator."

"But you're Mrs. Fable," said Henry.

"Now, you may call me Hope. It is your job to get through this book about—"

"History," Henry finished for her.

"Yes, history. It's everybody's story. And now, it's your story, Henry. You are a Tale Traveler. I cannot walk with you. But I can help you along. It is your job to follow these stories to their endings. It is my job to help you reach those endings without damaging them. I will appear to you when you need help, and don't worry. I am reading right along with you so I will know when those times come."

"But how do I get out?" Henry was eager to know.

"When you've reached the last adventure in this book, you will see the way. It's a story, Henry. All you have to do is read between the lines," said Hope in a slow, deliberate voice; and with that, she was gone.

"Hope, wait!" said Henry. His voice was lost in the noise as the crowds around him were again moving and speaking. He turned back toward them not knowing what to do or think. He repeated Hope's advice to himself: "All you have to do is read between the lines." Henry looked more closely at the crowds in front of the castle. They were in lines—two long lines. Between those two lines, at the front of the castle, a large parchment was posted. Henry ran up to the sign and read it.

His Majesty *King Ferdinand*
and
Her Majesty *Queen Isabella*

Having recently conquered Granada,
do hereby welcome

Christopher Columbus

to their court to discuss
a maritime exploration.

"Chris! Chris, there you are!" said a man running to Henry's side. Henry looked on with lost eyes. He didn't know what he had just read or who this man was. "Chris, it's me, your little brother! Bartholomew! Bart!" Still, Henry said nothing. "We don't have time for games now, Chris. The king and queen are waiting for you!"

"For me?" Henry exclaimed as he snapped out of it. "Chris? Christopher Columbus? Oh no! No, you must have the wrong person. I'm Henry. I'm only ten years old! This is a mistake."

"Ten years old? Come on, Chris," said Bart. "I know you're nervous, but we can do this. You and I have both made maps, and I just worked with a great maritime navigator in Africa. Spain has money to spare this time, so I know they can afford to send you on this mission. I know we can show them that by traveling west, we can reach the east. Maybe even India! We could bring back spices and make everybody rich . . . including us!"

Before he had time to think about what had just happened, Henry found himself standing in front of the king and queen on their thrones. His brother, or rather, Christopher Columbus' brother, had bowed deeply. Henry simply stared ahead in shock. A real king and a real queen were right there in front of him! And they were staring back at him too! They wore no expression. Or maybe they did. Were they mad? Why were they mad at him? Henry was confused.

"Psst!" Bart whispered loudly. "Christopher!"

"What?" Henry said louder than he meant to.

Bart cleared his throat and indicated with a nod that Henry needed to bow.

"Oh! Oh, Your Majesties, forgive me!" Henry quickly spat out while he bowed as deeply as he could. "I just thought you were so cool!"

"It's nearly August, Mr. Columbus. Nobody is cool," said the queen in an angry tone.

"No, I mean," Henry scrambled, "you guys are like a real king and queen. That is so bad, man!"

"Bad?" asked King Ferdinand. "It appears the great mariner Christopher Columbus has a problem with royalty."

"What are you doing?" Bart asked in an angry whisper.

"No. I mean. Um . . ." Henry bowed again to the king and queen. "I'm sorry, sirs. I mean, Your Majesties. I'm just nervous."

"Well, you've been bothering us for eight years, Mr. Columbus. Don't start with nerves now. What is it this time?" questioned Queen Isabella.

"This isn't more of that business about the world not being flat, is it?" added King Ferdinand.

"Flat? Of course it's not flat! The world is round! Everybody knows that!" Henry laughed out loud.

"I beg your pardon!" exclaimed the queen.

"What my brother means to say, Your Majesty, is that we are expert chart makers. My brother and I are both experienced mariners. We believe that the Enterprise of the Indies—"

"Hey, I've heard of that!" Henry said excitedly. Bart, the king, and the queen looked at Henry strangely; and all fell silent. He felt silly for a moment but decided he'd better go on. "I mean, of course I've heard of that. I named it. I came up with the Enterprise of the Indies because *I am* Christopher Columbus! I get it now!"

Suddenly, Henry came to know that in this story, he wouldn't just get to read, but he would actually be living it—as the main character. What was stranger still was that he now found his mind to be filled with facts and knowledge that could only belong to Christopher Columbus.

Henry then noticed that they were all still staring at him.

"I'm sure what my brother is trying to say . . ." Bart began.

"No, Bart, I've got it now. It's okay. You see, Your Majesties, we have been coming to you for eight years because it is our hope to bring spices and great riches to Spain." (The words came easily to Henry.) "John II of Portugal has already turned down this chance, and we are returning to you. I believe that if you could just help pay for my crew and my ships and a few supplies, we could make this journey. I believe so strongly in this that I am willing to risk my own life to prove that the world is not flat. I will sail west out of the Canary Islands, and after just a short time, I feel sure that my crew will reach India. If I am successful, this will save Spain time and money when trading with India. Please think about it this time."

"Very well," said Queen Isabella. "But only because I don't want to keep seeing you back here for another eight years!"

"And you have to find your own crew," added the king.

"Thank you!" said Henry.

"Thank you, Your Majesties!" exclaimed Bart, and the two of them left happily.

CHAPTER 4

Turning the Page

"HOPE!" HENRY CALLED once he was outside. "Hope, come back! I did it!"

"Who's Hope?" Bart said as he ran out of the castle behind Henry.

Henry turned toward him and saw Bart suddenly stop running in the middle of the air! He had frozen along with the rest of the scene. That could only mean one thing.

"Hey, Narrator Lady!" Henry called loudly while looking around.

Henry began to wander about the grounds, weaving his way through frozen pedestrians. The people looked like wax statues. Cautiously, he reached out and touched the face of one man. His skin was soft and warm, but he didn't move at all when Henry touched him. It was a scary feeling. Henry shivered and pulled his hand away. He continued to pass through the stillness around him. Henry saw a small bird in flight. It looked like it was suspended by a string. He passed his hand over the bird in amazement, imagining that he would catch whatever it was that held it in midair. His fingers closed together on nothing.

Next, he approached a woman carrying a large wooden bucket of water. The light shone upon the water, and its glassy surface looked like a darkly tinted mirror. Henry looked up at the young woman. She was as lifeless as all of the other statuelike figures near the castle. He put his hand out to touch her cheek and remembered the spooky feeling of brushing against the man's skin, so he withdrew his fingers before completing the action.

The young woman's bucket seemed safe enough. Henry dipped his fingers into the water, suddenly realizing he was thirsty after his strange adventures of the day. The water didn't feel the way he had expected. His fingers didn't seem wet; and as his hand passed deeper into the bucket, he experienced a static, tingling sensation. It reminded Henry of putting his hand close to the surface of a television that has been on for a long time. He cupped some of the water in his hand and poured it into his mouth. He felt it slide coolly down his throat and into his stomach but still wasn't sure he had actually taken a drink. Henry looked again into the bucket, to get a more satisfying drink, when he realized something. Normally, rings of ripples would have appeared on the surface of the water in the bucket when he had dipped his hand into it, but the liquid remained still. Henry peered curiously into the odd bucket of water and saw something stranger still.

When Henry woke in the morning and looked into his mirror, he saw himself staring back. Henry didn't look that different when compared to any other Midwest American preteenaged boy. His light skin and the few scattered freckles always appeared darker after a day in the sun. Like most boys nowadays though, he never did get enough of this. He'd rather play at video games than athletics. So he kept his few fair freckles and an even fairer complexion. His eyes were light, golden brown, with eyebrows to match and long black lashes. Henry had a nose his face still hadn't quite grown into and youthful cheeks that were still chubby enough for the unwanted pinches by annoying older relatives. Henry's smile, when he shared it, was a wide, toothy grin behind big round lips. Beneath his unkempt sandy brown hair, just short enough to avoid the barber, was a pair of uneven, stick-out ears. You could usually find Henry wearing oversized T-shirts along with a pair of baggy jeans that his mother ensured was worn with a belt. On his large dragging feet was a pair of gym shoes that looked like they belonged in the trash sometime ago. Henry blended in with the other boys his age and, looking as he did, could have just as easily fit in at the skate park as he did at the arcade.

Looking into the bucket though, Henry did not see that familiar reflection in the water. Instead, there was a grown man with much darker skin than that of Henry. His eyes were dark, and he even had some facial hair. Henry saw the ruffles of the white shirt around his neck and grimaced. The man in the bucket grimaced too. The rest of the reflection was blurry. As he leaned in closer, a small pebble dropped into the bucket. Henry stood up quickly and backed away from the woman. She still hadn't moved at all. He looked around again as though he had forgotten where he was for a moment.

"Who did that?" he asked as his heart skipped a beat. "Hope?"

"Over here," called the Narrator.

Henry walked in the direction of Hope's voice, near an outer wall around the castle.

"Hello?" he said curiously.

"Look up, dear," the voice came again.

Henry looked up, way up. At the very top of the wall sat the Narrator, reading a book as calmly as if she were sitting on a park bench on the ground.

"Hope," he shouted upward, "is that you?"

"Well, I'm certainly not a bird," she replied.

"How'd you do that?"

"Do what?"

"Get way up there?"

"Oh, there's a lot I can do that you don't know yet!" She laughed.

"I can barely hear you!" shouted Henry.

"Of course," said Hope. "How rude of me." With that, she clapped her hands twice, and out of nowhere, Henry felt a strong wind at his back. He turned toward the breeze. It looked like the entire castle was blowing over onto him. In fact, it looked like all of the people were blowing over too! Suddenly, Henry saw what was happening. It was a giant page, and it was turning—with him still on it! He was going to get squashed!

"You'd best come up here with me, Henry," the Narrator calmly said. She clapped again. Henry wasn't sure whether he had jumped or been pushed by the page or been pulled by Hope, but the next thing he knew was that he was by her side at the top of the wall. The scene below him had changed too. It was completely blank as if it had been erased or maybe not even written yet. Hope was still dressed in the clothing of 1492, and in her hair she wore a pencil that looked as worn as the old books in the Valders Town Library, and it had a large golden eraser.

"Whoa!" said Henry. "Wicked!"

"Now, young Tale Traveler, you were doing just fine. Whatever did you call me for?"

"I did it! I got the king and queen to let me, I mean, to let Christopher Columbus, take his trip," Henry replied excitedly. "I don't even know how I did it! Hey, how did I do it? How did I know all that stuff?"

"Well, you figured out that you will be participating in the stories. That's a good start. When you become the different characters in the tales of *History*, you will have that person's memories and knowledge and thoughts as well as your own," Hope explained to Henry.

"And I look like them too, don't I?" Henry exclaimed.

"For a little while, yes," she replied.

"I didn't get to see everything though," he complained. "I know my skin is darker. I'm Spanish?" he asked.

"Italian, actually," said Hope. "And that's about all we know. There was never an authentic portrait of Christopher Columbus found. That's not really what matters right now though. As for this story, you are not done, Henry. You've barely begun. You don't remember Christopher Columbus for visiting a king and queen, do you?"

"Well, no," he admitted.

"You remember him for making a voyage to the New World, right?" she questioned.

"Yes, but . . ." He stopped.

"Well then," she said, "I guess you'd better get started on that."

"I don't know how," Henry said.

"Let's see," said Hope. She began paging through the book in her hand, and Henry realized it was exactly the same as the book he had gotten pulled into back in the small room of the library. Well, not exactly the same since this one fit in her hand, and instead of saying *History* on the cover, it read *Henry's History*. However, this was the same book. Henry was certain of that.

"Here we go," said Hope. "King Ferdinand said you need to find your own crew. That means ships too. Here's the page you're on now." Henry peered over her shoulder and caught a glimpse of what looked like a waterfront carnival. He tried to make out the words on the page, but the Narrator was too quick for him as she pulled the pencil from her hair and began erasing the words and picture.

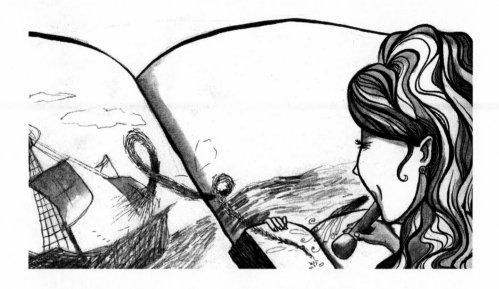

"What are you doing?" Henry exclaimed. "Stop!"

Hope had erased the entire page. She then blew the eraser dust off of her book and onto the blank pages below them. A busy scene erupted onto the pages below, and although it wasn't moving yet, Henry could tell that it was full of life. He could also tell that it wasn't a carnival but a real-life port full of ships and traders. He supposed that a seaport must have been the closest thing to a mall that existed in the year 1492. At that moment, Henry wondered if he could get out of his red robe and into something that didn't make him feel like a girl.

"Well done!" Hope said in a proud way. "Wish I could join you, but this is where you take back over!" she said with a smile, and she winked one big emerald green eye deeply. Then, as quickly as she had appeared, she was gone again.

CHAPTER 5

The Three Ships

T HE SCENE BELOW came to life, and everybody was moving and talking. The water was splashing against long wooden piers beneath him. The waves looked so rough that he could almost imagine them moving. Wait a minute! He wasn't imagining. In place of the castle wall he had been sitting on top of was now a very tall mast of a ship, and there Henry sat at the very tip-top of it, clinging to the mast just below the crow's nest. At least, there Henry slipped, slid, bounced, and bobbled at the very tip-top of it.

"Aahh!" Henry half gasped and half screamed.

"Chris, what do you think?" said Bart's voice from very far below Henry on the deck of the ship. From up here, Bart seemed very small.

"It's, um, great," said Henry nervously as he wrapped his arms and legs tightly around the rope at the top of the pole. "Just great." He clung on for dear life wondering how he would ever get down from here.

If he wasn't so frightened, he would have been excited to look at the beautiful ship he was on. It had three tall masts with square sails and was long and thin. It looked something like what Henry would expect for a pirate ship, except that the sails were all bright white and red and there were no men walking around with eye patches, wooden legs, or hooks for hands.

"So we'll take her?" asked Bart. "She's called the *Pinta!*"

"Yes!" Henry answered. His voice shook as he spoke. He hoped Bart wouldn't notice how scared he sounded.

"Come on down then!" Bart called up.

"I can't!" Henry yelled back. His heart was beating so hard in his chest that he thought it felt like a motor that was revving up to take a speedy trip right out of his body through his throat.

"What?" Bart shouted.

"What I mean is, um, it's my robe, Bart," Henry lied while trying to think of some way out of this very steep mess he'd gotten into. "My robe is stuck in the ropes."

"Not a problem!" Henry heard from a man's voice directly beneath him who was climbing quickly. "Funny way to meet, no?"

"And you are?" asked Henry as the man scurried up alongside him so that both of them were at the top of the mast together.

"Martin Alonso Pinzon. I am captain here on the *Pinta*. I would be honored to sail with you. You are not alone in this belief that we can sail to the west, Mr. Columbus," said the sailor. The man held on to the mast like a monkey, not at all upset by how high off the water and ground the two were.

"Oh well, I'm honored to sail with you too, Señor Pinzon," said Henry. He tried to fake a confident smile.

"Please call me Marty," he said as he fumbled with Henry's robe. "I don't think you're stuck, sir."

"I'm not?" Henry pretended to be surprised.

"No. I see no snag here. We'll take the fast way down," Marty replied calmly.

"What's that?" Henry asked. Before Marty answered, Henry found out what the fast way was. Marty pulled a knot out of the rope that Henry held, and the two of them rode the rope all the way down to the deck of the ship like a fast-dropping elevator.

"All right then, Marty!" Henry said after feeling himself to make sure he was still in one piece after his ride. "It looks like you'll be joining us. Assemble your crew. We leave on the third day of August. My brother and I will go on to gather more ships."

"Glad to be aboard!" said the captain, shaking Henry's hand firmly. Henry and Bart began to leave the deck of the *Pinta* for the pier in search of more ships and captains to join them on their Enterprise of the Indies.

"Hold on there!" called Marty before they had made it off of his ship.

"What is it?" Henry and Bart said in unison.

"I have a brother too. He is named Vicente Yañez Pinzon, and you can find him just a short distance down the waterfront here. He has a ship too. She's called the *Niña*. It's smaller than my vessel but has four tall masts with triangle sails. You can't miss it," Marty said as he pointed out the direction Henry and Bart should go along the coastal port to find the *Niña*. The two of them nodded in thanks to Marty and began walking toward Marty's brother.

After Henry had met Vicente and enlisted the *Niña*, he decided it was time to find one more ship to go on the voyage. He knew this was what Christopher Columbus would have done. Together, he and Bart walked back and forth along the coast until a large cargo ship docked that caught Henry's eye.

"I just don't think this is our day." Bart began. "I don't see any ship that will do for—"

"That's the one!" Henry interrupted, cutting off his brother's words.

"Chris, it's a cargo ship. Isn't it a little large for this trip?" asked Bart.

"No!" Henry exclaimed. "No, it's not. This is the one *I* want to pilot."

Henry knew then how Christopher Columbus must have felt when he first laid eyes on the *Santa Maria*. She was a huge ship. Henry had seen pictures in books and on his computer, but they did not prepare him for the large size of the *Santa Maria*. The ship came to a point at the front and had large colorful shields painted along the sides. The back of the ship was seventy-two feet off the top of the water and also had shields decorating its sides. It was almost a hundred feet from the front of the ship to the back. That means almost twenty men could have lain flat on their backs on the deck from the front to the back of the ship. The sails were enormous. The man showing them the *Santa Maria* told Henry that there were two thousand seven hundred feet of canvas making those sails and over four thousand feet of rope holding them up! One of the large sails had a big red cross painted on the center of it, and the mast in the middle of the ship went sixty-five feet into the air off the deck of the ship, and at the very top was a small basket called a crow's nest where a sailor could be a lookout. It would have taken four or five big houses stacked on top of each other to reach from the surface of the water to the top of the tallest mast. Later, Henry also saw beneath the deck of the ship where there was room to sleep and store supplies for the trip. Henry would even have his own sleeping quarters with a private set of stairs up to the deck.

The *Santa Maria* was the neatest thing Henry had ever seen in his entire life. On August 3, he would join Marty with the *Pinta* and Vicente with the *Niña* to sail to the New World, and he would be leading as captain of the *Santa Maria*. He couldn't wait!

CHAPTER 6

Voyage to the New World

I T WAS THE morning of August 3, 1492. HENRY was glad to finally be out of the red robe and ruffled shirt he had arrived in. He was now wearing a plain colored shirt and pants that went just below his knees. His shoes were wider and flatter. Today, he would set sail. Vicente gave the *Niña* square sails to match the *Pinta* and the *Santa Maria*. Marty had helped to find crews for all of the ships, and they were all ready to go.

The ships were being untied and pushed out from the docks by their crews using long ropes, wooden poles, and small side boats as well as some men on foot in the shallower waters. Henry looked back and noticed Bart still on the shore with a beautiful woman that looked like a princess to him. She was dressed in a pretty green velvet gown with lace sleeves, and she wore a large veiled hat. He headed back to see why Bart wasn't on board the *Santa Maria*.

"Bart, aren't you coming?" Henry asked.

"No, sorry, Chris. This is your trip, brother," Bart said.

"Who's the girl?" Henry whispered.

"Very funny!" Bart exclaimed. "It's your wife, Doña Filipa Perestrello e Moniz."

"Wife? Eew!" Henry said.

"What?" said the woman. "Eew?"

"I mean, ooh. Ooh, how pretty you look," Henry quickly replied.

"That's better," she smiled. "Bart and I got you something from one of the traders. We hope you like it."

Doña Filipa reached into a small purse covered with jewels and pulled out a chain. On the chain was a small charm of the letter *A*.

"Why is it the letter *A*?" Henry asked.

"*A* stands for *Admiral*," said the woman. "If you succeed, King Ferdinand may make you admiral of the sea."

"I thought it should have been *B* for *Bart*," said Bart jokingly. "I don't want you to forget who helped to get you here."

"I'll never forget you," said Henry. "You're my brother!"

"Be safe," said Doña Filipa as she put the chain around his neck. She then kissed his cheek. Henry blushed.

"Good luck, big bro," said Bart, and he shook Henry's hand.

Then Henry ran back out into the water to continue dragging the *Santa Maria* away from the docks with his men. When the ships were far enough out to float on their own, the captains and their crews climbed aboard on long rope ladders lowered from the decks, and they began their mission to sail to India.

The Atlantic Ocean somehow looked bigger from this side of the world, Henry thought. He had seen it once from New York City with his family. He thought for a moment about his mom and dad and about his sisters and brother.

"They'll be all right, you know," said a familiar voice.

"Hello, Hope," said Henry. He noticed that the scene had frozen again. "Who will be all right?"

"Your family will. I'm reading along, remember? I always know what you're thinking."

"Oh, that's right," Henry said.

"Your brother is facing gods and goddesses, monsters and legends on an . . . odyssey of sorts in *Michael's Mythology* right now. Hope smiled slightly as she said the words. At this moment, Fay is serving with the legendary Robin Hood in *Fay's Fairy Tales;* and Patty, through the eyes of Pocahontas, is discovering life in *Patty's Pioneer Days*," Hope told Henry. "Meanwhile, we're learning what the world would have been like without the great Thomas Edison, thanks to *Sam's Science* and—unfortunately—a little unwanted help from a man named Des." She stopped. "Oh, you haven't met Sam yet or, thankfully, Des. No doubt you will one day. My point is that the other Tale Travelers are all doing just fine."

"What about Mom and Dad?" he asked.

"They won't miss you at all. When you are a Tale Traveler, the world outside sort of slows down, just like when you're reading any good book. When you return from *History*, it will feel as though mere moments have passed for them," the Narrator explained. "They don't notice that time has slowed just as you and Michael didn't notice the change when your sisters went into their books. And nobody at all noticed when Sam went into his book. I even know of two people who went into books and spent lifetimes with nobody knowing they were gone."

"Who?" he asked.

"A story for another time, Henry," Hope sighed sweetly.

Henry stared sadly down at the water below. It was as still as the bucket of water belonging to the woman near the castle. As he gazed at the perfect calm, he huffed out deeply at the unfamiliar, unclear reflection of Christopher Columbus.

"And you'll get your reflection back too . . . eventually. That, however, will take a little more work." She winked at him. There was something so childlike in the Narrator's green eyes. He was starting to count on the wink Hope so often shared. It made him feel immediately better.

"I never thought I'd miss a real mirror." Henry laughed as he removed his hat, ruffled his own hair, and replaced the hat. "Hey, are you going to do that page-turning thing now? It's time to be across the ocean by now, isn't it?"

"Do you think I would let you miss the journey?" She smiled.

"Oh, man!" Henry grumbled.

"I know what I can do though," said Hope. "Have a good trip. Oh! And hold on to that little charm from your wife!"

"She's not my wife!" Henry laughed back at her.

The Narrator disappeared, and Henry felt that familiar strong breeze at his back. The sails puffed out their chests like proud fathers of the journey before him; and with a deep, happy breath, Henry felt the *Santa Maria* gain speed.

"Thanks, Hope," he whispered into the air, knowing that the wind was the help she provided.

Within moments, the *Niña*, the *Pinta*, and the *Santa Maria* at the front had all opened their sails. Wind filled the many thousands of feet of canvas, and all three ships were skimming along on the top of the sea as if they had motors behind them. Knowing that his family was fine made it okay for Henry to enjoy this moment. He stood at the front of his ship and felt the salty air blowing against his face. This would be a great trip!

As the days and weeks passed, Henry was glad that the Narrator didn't turn the page and let him miss the ride. The days were very long because there was sun from the early hours to the very latest hours. Every day they saw new types of animals. Dolphins, whales, and even sharks appeared from time to time. They went fishing and ate every type of fish Henry could imagine plus a few he had never heard of. There were no girls on the ship at all, so when they finished eating, they could even burp and wipe their hands and faces on their shirts! At night the skies were filled with stars and the water seemed to stand still. The stars and moon reflected on the ocean, and Henry would imagine he was floating in the sky, somewhere out in space.

His crew became his friends, and they would tell stories at night and dream about what they would do once they reached the west and found spices and riches. A few men on the crew still didn't believe the world was round. Sometimes they would fight about what could happen if the world dropped off at the end of the trip. But even the men that thought the world was flat weren't afraid of making the voyage. They believed they were such good sailors that they could turn the ship around when they reached the end of the world.

Henry believed they were good sailors too. They were always tying knots, untying knots, opening sails, closing sails, and even turning the sails. The idea was to catch the wind so that it would push the ship west. When the *Santa Maria* would make a change, Henry could walk to the back of the ship and watch the *Niña* and the *Pinta* do the same thing with their sails so that they could follow right behind Henry's ship. Marty and Vicente knew what they were doing, and Henry was glad he had them as captains.

Henry also learned new words from the sailors. Instead of the ship having a front, it had a *bow*. Instead of a back, the ship had a *stern*. The right side of the *Santa Maria* was called *starboard* and the left side was *port*. Also, instead of radios or phones and computer maps, they used stars, telescopes, compasses, and hand-drawn charts to guide them. Then they would fly flags of different colors to tell the two ships behind them what they should do next to stay on path with and out of the wake of the *Santa Maria*.

Since he had Christopher Columbus' thoughts, he knew what he needed to know in order to captain the *Santa Maria*. As Henry though, he was very impressed with how much Christopher Columbus and the other sailors could do in a world without motors or computers. Henry was sure that there was nothing his crew could not handle.

CHAPTER 7

The Storm

HENRY WOKE UP one morning on the ship, and he was cold! He pulled on a coat over his clothes. It was dark too. *The sun should be up by now,* Henry thought. He peered up the stairs from his quarters expecting to see something blocking the entrance and the sunlight. Instead, the face of one of his sailors came into view.

"Captain!" the voice shouted to Henry from the deck of the ship. "Captain, I think you need to see this!" It was Rodrigo de Triana. Rodrigo was the lookout for the *Santa Maria* and was always the first to see if there was something important coming ahead for the ship. Henry tried to imagine something great. Maybe this would be the day that Rodrigo would call out, "Tierra! Tierra!" the word that means *land* in Spanish.

Henry rushed up the steps to the deck of the ship. There was no land in sight. Instead, in the sky ahead of the *Santa Maria*, Henry could see clouds—*dark* clouds. He turned around and looked at the sky in all directions. There was no escaping the storm. Henry could see clouds everywhere he looked. It was as if night was closing in on the three ships in a big circle, squeezing them into total darkness. For the first time since he left for the voyage, Henry felt scared.

Looking around the ship, Henry noticed all of his crewmates also staring up at the skies. He had to act quickly. They were waiting for his command to prepare for what was coming. This snapped Henry out of his daze. It was getting dark quickly and the lanterns that light the decks of the ship were not lit because it was early in the morning. "Light the lamps!" he shouted. "Light the lamps while we still can!"

Men began running from one end of the deck to the other lighting lanterns along the way. At the rate those dark clouds were moving in, everything would soon be black. Then there would be no chance for them to make it through this storm. It didn't seem like any time at all had passed before Henry felt the winds pick up, and he was sure it wasn't Hope this time. The *Santa Maria* began rocking every which way. Henry felt ill. He wanted to stop rocking, to be on dry land, to be rescued and not be the rescuer. He looked up and saw all of the sails open.

"The sails!" Henry shouted to his men. "Lower the sails!" Henry knew that if the sails were open during a storm, the wind could blow the ship in places that he knew nothing about. The ship could blow somewhere that there were no charts for. Worst of all, it could blow the ships back in the direction they came from.

Henry knew that it was up to him to finish Christopher Columbus' mission. If they blew backward, he would have even farther to travel. Plus, he didn't want to be out at sea any longer. If he had to eat fish for one more day, he knew he'd get sick. They were working furiously for almost an hour, at full speed and doing lots of lifting and heavy work preparing the ship and protecting the supplies. His exhausted mind began to wander. He imagined a piece of pizza with lots of cheese and pepperoni.

SMACK!

Henry's daydream was broken by a frozen splash of water that had come up over the side of the ship.

"Captain!" called a man from the base of the masts. "Help us!"

Henry shook off his sleepy daze and ran over to his men as they tried to lower the heavy sails. The wind, rain, and sea began to put out the lamps they had lit and cold darkness began to take over. There wasn't much time now. They had to get the sails down. The strong breezes were lifting up water and spraying it in their faces like a fire hose. It hurt, and it made it very hard to loosen the ropes that were holding up the sails. Finally, they had untied the ropes holding up the largest center sail. As they lowered it, Henry noticed that the beautiful red cross that had been painted in its middle had torn. There was no time to feel sad about this though. There were more sails to lower. He and the crew tied down the main sail.

Henry ran to another sail to help more men. The storm was raging now. He felt water being sprayed at him from the ocean and hail began to pour down from the sky. He could no longer tell which way was up or from where the storm was coming. The hail bounced all over the deck of the ship. The *Santa Maria* was rocking back and forth and from side to side. Henry kept falling down as he was trying to reach his men. He grabbed on to a pole to keep his balance when he reached another sail. Just as he grabbed on, a fast wind swept the whole pole backward with Henry still on it. He hung out over the surface of the water for one frantic moment. Then a gust swept the pole back over the deck of the ship. Another sailor was knocked to the ground. Henry held on with all his might, but a third gust of wind grabbed him and tossed him down onto the deck as well.

Where are you, Hope? Henry wondered.

Henry got up and saw that the sail he was in charge of was the last one still up. His men had managed to tie down all of the other sails and were now taking shelter in a huddle at the bow of the ship. The rocking of the *Santa Maria* had subsided for a moment. Henry called for one of his crew. The fallen sailor staggered to his feet, and together they managed to tie down the last sail before the wind picked up yet again. It was just in time. Now, the bow of the ship rocked dozens of feet into the air and slammed down upon the water. The force threw one of the men right off the front of the ship!

"Man overboard!" was yelled. "Help, Captain! Man overboard!"

Against the pelting baseball-sized hail chunks, covering his face with his arms as he moved, Henry forced his way to the front of the ship, barely able to tell which way was which anymore in the chaos of the raging storm and sea. He peered over the edge in the now almost pitch blackness. His crewmate had held on to the frame of one of the shields on the side of the bow.

"I've got you!" Henry cried as he reached one hand down over the front of the ship and felt feverishly for the hand of the sailor who had fallen overboard. It was Juan, the youngest man on his crew.

Henry's fingers were soaked and cold. It was hard to hold on to Juan. Henry hooked his ankles around wooden bars over the edge of the ship and lowered himself toward Juan in order to get a better grip on his crewmate. He hung on to the edge of the boat by his feet and reached down his second hand. As he was stretched out over the side of the ship, another huge wave rocked the boat thirty feet up into the air and back down onto the ocean surface. Then a huge chunk of ice slammed into the side of Henry's forehead. His head jerked backward, and Henry watched as his chain fell from his neck and into the wild, stormy sea below. He was dazed, and everything went blurry. He began to feel Juan's fingers slipping away, when . . .

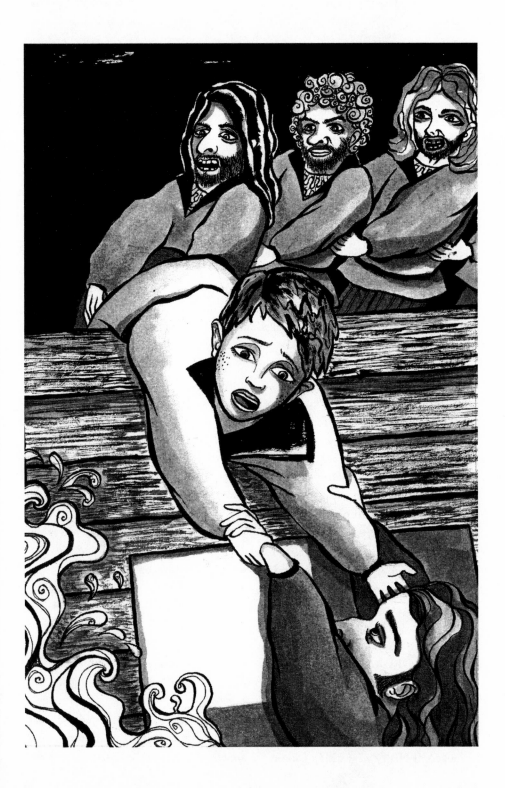

"Hang on, Captain!" came the voices of a dozen men behind him. They had formed a human chain and were together pulling Henry and Juan aboard. He groggily tightened his fingers on Juan as the two were raised.

Once on board, the men gathered at the center of the deck because there was nothing left that they could do to control the *Santa Maria* in the storm. The men tied themselves together and huddled against the base of the center mast.

Henry stumbled dizzily to the stern of the ship. He saw the *Pinta* being tossed about on the water, but she looked like she was doing all right.

"Marty!" Henry screamed out over the sea to his friend on the *Pinta*. It was no use, of course. The rain and waves around him echoed loudly in his clogged and frostbitten ears. Henry could barely hear his own voice, and the *Pinta* was too far to speak to even when the weather was calm. He felt helpless.

The *Niña* was nowhere to be seen. It was useless against the sounds of the storm to try and spot her. Henry hoped that Vicente and the crew of the *Niña* would be okay. Suddenly, a large bolt of lightning cracked in the distance and lit up the shape of the *Niña* like a ghost ship. Her sails were all safely down. *Thank goodness,* thought Henry. Now, all three ships had at least a *chance* of surviving.

Henry tied himself together with his men, and they all waited and hoped for the storm to pass. Another severe gust extinguished the very last lantern. Henry couldn't even tell whether or not his own eyes were open. He and the *Santa Maria* crew were all soaking wet and freezing. He put his arm around a very frightened young Juan.

"We'll be okay," Henry assured him. "We're good sailors." But as he said these words, Henry began to cry. Even if they could see, his men would never know because his tears blended in with the rain streaking his scared, tired, beaten face.

That night, instead of talking about what they would do if they found riches at the end of their voyage, they talked about what they would do if they could just make it through the storm. Then, for a long time, nobody spoke at all. Henry and the crew held on to one another for warmth and safety, but mostly for comfort.

Somewhere between scared talks about the storm, the long followed silence, and hopeful dreams about surviving, the *Santa Maria* crew fell asleep one at a time. Henry stayed awake. He knew it was what Christopher Columbus would have done.

First, the pounding hail stopped, then the winds calmed, and the sea stopped spraying onto the deck of the ship. Finally, just before dawn, Henry began to spot a few stars. Then, at last, he saw the sun rise over the sea. A full day had passed since Henry put on his coat to keep warm. The storm had ended.

Henry looked at his now-ragged crew. Their clothes were torn, twisted, wet and stained with the salt of the ocean. Juan was sleeping, and Henry realized how young he looked. If Henry were still in Chicago, Juan would be about the age of some of the boys he had challenged in the arcade. Yet here Juan was exploring the world in a time hundreds of years before video games were even imagined.

Henry no longer thought his crew could handle anything. He knew it. He also knew that he could handle it with them, and he felt proud.

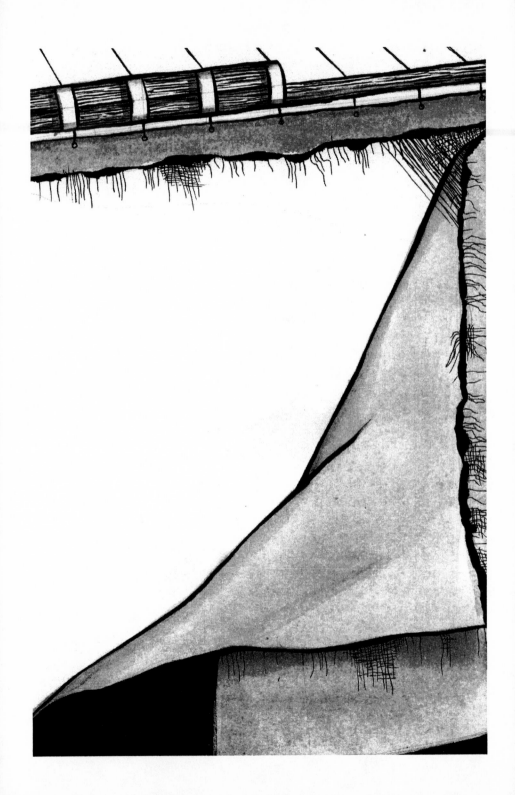

CHAPTER 8

The Long, Cold, Wet Misery

WHEN THE SKY was clear and Henry and his men were rested and ready to take care of the destruction on the ship, he realized how much his face hurt. Henry imagined he couldn't have been much of a sight when he reached up and felt the dried blood on his forehead from where the huge piece of hail had hit him the night before. At least, he thought it had been hail. It could just as easily have been a piece of his own ship. He'd never really know. He tried not to think about the stinging in his cut. There was too much work to be done.

It took a full day to clean the *Santa Maria* from the storm. The *Pinta* and the *Niña* took two days. Because they were smaller, the storm must have done more damage to them. They were tossed about more freely on the water, being ravaged all the while.

On the *Santa Maria*, the wood on some of the masts had begun to split. The cracks were small, so Henry wasn't worried about them being able to hold up the sails. Tar was used to patch and seal wood on the deck and in the masts. The ropes were in good shape, so that was one less thing that Henry and his crew had to fix.

The large center sail had to be sewn. One man on the crew was an expert at sail mending, so that was not a problem. Henry even offered his red robes for patching. He was glad to be rid of them because they still looked like a dress to him.

The deck of the ship was covered in unmelted hail pellets and dried sea plants. As the hail melted, it left ugly white circles on the surface of the ship. The plants stuck to the deck as if they had been glued on. The salt from the sea left the *Santa Maria* looking dusty once it finally dried. Much of the paint on the shields was cracked and chipped by the hail. Since some of the hail stones were large, there were small pieces of splintered and dented wood on parts of the deck and sides of the ship.

Henry's feet were still cold and swollen from the storm. His shoes were drenched, and they rubbed the backs of his heels raw. He wanted to take them off. He was sure he felt at least one blister on the back of a heel, but he had to wear those saturated, squishy shoes because if he didn't, he would get slivers or infections from walking on the damaged deck of the *Santa Maria*. He couldn't even change into another pair because most of his supplies had been soaked.

In fact, his personal things were not the only things wet. Much of the crew had lost important things, and the biggest loss of all was food.

Henry and his crew ate plenty of seafood on the trip, but they had also brought other things to help stay healthy. Most of the fresh fruit and vegetables had gone bad before the storm. The grain had been okay though until the rains came. Now, all of it was ruined, and the few spices they had were completely destroyed. Spices were the one thing that made eating so much of the same food for two months bearable. Even worse is that many of the fresh water barrels tipped or broke and spilled during the storm. Henry thought it was strange that they had to ration water in the middle of the ocean, but the salt water wasn't healthy for him and his crew to drink, so they had brought barrels of fresh water along on the journey.

Some of Henry's men were sick after the storm, and having no fresh food and very little water from storage below deck made it hard to get them healthy again. The ship's medical supplies were running low too. Henry had some of the crew that were feeling well begin collecting and cleaning sea plants to feed to the men who were ill so that they could get better. The sea plants tasted awful, and they had no spices left to cover the flavor. The crew did what they had to do in order to keep going though, and sea plants had some of the vitamins they needed.

When the ships began to sail again, Henry did not feel the same joy as when he had left for this voyage in August. The ships could not move as quickly after the damage from the storms. The main sail of the *Santa Maria* did not catch the wind as well, and steering the ship was hard. Sometimes, the *Santa Maria* would finally pick up the pace only to have to slow down for the *Niña* or the *Pinta* to catch up. Henry thought about the size of the *Santa Maria* and sometimes wished he had a smaller sailing ship instead of the large cargo one he picked. Maybe Bart had been right.

When the ships did speed more quickly, Henry no longer liked standing at the bow to feel the breezes. The salty air was cold and sharp against his face which burned with his injury from the storm. His nose, lips, and forehead were dry; and his skin was chapped. He didn't like the feel of the wind, and the smell of damp air only made him miss land more. His clothes felt itchy against his skin, and his hair had grown long and was always blowing into his eyes or sticking to his still-healing wound. He turned his back to the wind and faced the stern. This was no help as the sight of the *Santa Maria*, so neglected now that it looked something like a ghost ship, turned his stomach.

The crew didn't stay up at night and tell stories anymore. They did stay up, but Henry was not invited over to share in the talks they would have.

The sky wasn't always clear, and they rationed fuel so that lanterns could not be used for the whole night any longer. Sometimes, when the sun set, it was so dark that Henry couldn't even see his own hand in front of his face. It would remind him of the night of the storm. He could see his breath though. The nights were cold now. He would have given almost anything to have even his red velvet robes back again.

Henry and his men would wear coats over their clothes, wrap up in leather or canvas blankets, and keep warm together in the few corners of the ship that the wind didn't touch. It wasn't much help. Sometimes it was so cold he thought he'd shiver right out of his skin.

One night, Henry told his men they could have a fire on the deck of the ship in a large pot-shaped stove that looked to Henry like a cauldron that a witch would use for mixing potions. He went below to get his blanket, feeling his way in the darkness. He wrapped up and pulled a hat on over his frozen red ears. Henry knew that if his head was warm, his whole body would feel better. He began walking back up the steep, now-creaky wooden steps to the deck. The stairs to and from his quarters now seemed harder to climb than when he first came aboard. Henry was sure they would give way beneath the weight of his tired body.

Just before he made it out into the open from below deck, where he knew a warm stove awaited him with his men crowded around it, he began to hear their voices.

"You have to eat something!"

"More seaweed? Are you crazy? I've eaten so much of that stuff I feel like I could grow roots."

"Well, we have fish."

"Fish is the only thing I've eaten more of than the green junk from the ocean. I think I'll pass."

"I could go for eggs."

"And pork!"

"With a big bowl of oranges and dates."

"My wife makes delicious flatbread."

"If all of us get together when we get home to Spain, we could have a grand meal!"

"You mean *if* we get back to Spain."

"That's true."

"I think you'd better get used to fish and sea plants, mate."

"Never. I'd rather swim back to Spain!"

"Forget Spain. I'd just like to get to any land. A deserted island will do. One of those places where the sand feels like fire after a hot day in the sun."

"I like the idea of warmth, but I don't know about land. I'm not sure I'll remember how to walk without rocking to keep my balance at the same time."

"What if we never reach land at all?"

"I don't think we will. The captain doesn't have star charts for all the way out here."

"You think we'll have to turn back?"

"We'd never make it. We have no supplies left."

"I heard the captain telling Rodrigo that the trip has been over three thousand nautical miles so far."

"And there is no sign of land ahead. When I sailed on a mission around the southern tip of Africa, at least we could see something that told us where we were; another ship from time to time or even a bird reminded us that land was near. Out here, we're all alone . . . nothing but sky and sea."

"And storms and cold."

"I don't think he knows what he's doing."

"We'll die out here. We'll all die or we'll fall off at the end. No matter how well we sail, the *Santa Maria* has been so beaten up on this trip that I don't think we could turn her around when the world drops off."

"I thought you agreed that the world was round."

"I'm having second thoughts."

It went on for a couple of hours. Henry listened as the men argued about the worst fates that could await them. They all said bad things about Henry and the trip and the once-beautiful *Santa Maria*. Nobody stuck up for Henry, not even Juan whom he had saved from falling overboard. They complained about the food and the freezing and the lack of supplies. Henry slumped down on the steps and listened to his entire crew go on and on about how unhappy they were and how they wished they could leave or had never come at all.

Henry didn't know what to do. Were his men right? He really didn't know where he was. Even with Christopher Columbus' knowledge, he realized that there was no clear answer to his location right now. He had one thought to keep him going: Hope. If he was in real trouble, Hope would have come. This must be the way it really was for Columbus and his men. Henry thought they must have been pretty amazing people to make this journey over five hundred years ago.

Henry didn't join his men but slept shivering on the dark steps after falling asleep to his crew's unhappy tales. Every one of them was miserable, and all of it was his fault.

CHAPTER 9

Tierra! Tierra!

H ENRY WOKE UP early the next day and went to the bow of the ship to look out at the sea. The morning air was cool. He thought about his men from the night before and wondered what he could do to make any of it better. Food, supplies, and the appearance of land were not things he could control. Then he thought about the cold. That, Henry thought, he might be able to handle.

Henry changed direction of the *Santa Maria* from west to southwest. It was a small change, but he thought he could at least help to make the trip a little warmer for his crew. Then Henry thought that this must be how Christopher Columbus missed what is America today. If Christopher Columbus continued west, he would have landed on the coast of what became the United States. A small change to the southwest put Columbus in the islands just south of America though.

The *Pinta* and the *Niña* followed the change in direction made by the *Santa Maria*. Henry's men were still not sure that this made any difference, but they liked the idea that it may warm up.

It was October 11. The ships had been sailing for more than two months, and they were all very tired, including Henry.

It became a warmer day, and the wind was steady, so Henry lay down on the deck and tried to enjoy himself. He knew something that the other men did not. Tomorrow was October 12, and on that day, Christopher Columbus made land. He closed his eyes, and he smiled.

The men were all quiet, and the water was still. Maybe the water was too still. Henry listened closely. He couldn't hear the water or anything else. He opened his eyes one at a time. The scene was frozen. He jumped up excitedly.

"Hope!" Henry called out. "Hope, I know you're there! Come out!"

Henry ran back and forth on the long deck of the *Santa Maria* searching the ship. He looked down into the sea. He even climbed to the very top of the center mast and into the crow's nest. This didn't scare him anymore as it had the first day he was at the top of the *Pinta*. Now, climbing a mast was as simple as climbing the stairs for Henry. He understood the way Marty had done it so calmly back on the *Pinta*.

"Hope!" he called again when he'd reached the top. Rodrigo was there, as still as a statue.

The ship was clear except for his frozen crew, the sea was still, and there was no sign of the Narrator anywhere. He climbed back down. Where could she be?

Just then, Henry heard a high-pitched whistling sound. It came again and again. It was a short repeating screech, and it was coming closer. What was that? Henry ran back to the bow of the ship and looked all around. The whistle grew closer and sounded more like a long squeak. Then Henry saw it—a bird!

"A bird!" he said. He hadn't realized he could actually forget the sound of a bird calling. After two months with no such sound though, he honestly did. The bird was flying toward the ship. They must not be frozen after all, Henry thought. How was that possible? What about Rodrigo and the frozen crew?

The bird was almost to Henry now. It flew over his head, high above the *Santa Maria*, and circled back around. It had something in its beak. The bird flew back and forth over Henry and dropped what looked like a long string which fell down to Henry. He reached out over the edge of the ship and caught the string, except it wasn't a string at all. It was a chain, and on the chain was a small charm of the letter *A*. The chain and charm had gotten beaten and colored from salt and water damage, but Henry knew it was the chain he had lost in the storm.

Henry looked up at the bird. He felt like he was dreaming. The bird circled lower and lower over Henry and gracefully flew to the edge of the ship. As it reached out a claw to grab the ship, the claw turned into a toe, then the foot into a human foot, and slowly, the feathers into long silvery hair, and the wings into a flowing white gown, and finally, the face into a human face—Hope's face. The Narrator tiptoed down the edge of the ship, as though that edge was as steady and smooth as an escalator, and she gently sat.

"It's you!" Henry smiled. He couldn't stop himself from hugging her.

"Hello, Henry," said Hope. "Now, didn't I tell you not to lose your wife's gift?"

"She's not my wife!" He laughed while he still stared openmouthed at the amazing, enchanted Narrator. "How did you . . . How? I mean . . . um . . ."

"Didn't I tell you that there was a lot I could do that you didn't know yet, Henry? We've barely begun." Hope began to pick a stringy green sea plant from her mane of long hair. "It took me two days to find that, by the way, and I had to steal it away from a very grumpy squid."

"You did that as a bird?" Henry wondered.

"No. A dolphin," Hope said plainly.

Henry chuckled. "I won't lose it again. I promise."

"How are you, young Tale Traveler?" she asked him sincerely while she looked warmly down with her big eyes.

"Great, now that you're here!" he replied. Then without meaning to, Henry launched into a long list of the terrible things that made him so upset. "I'm so tired. It's been a long trip. The *Santa Maria* is barely holding together. We're starved for something other than salty wet weeds and fish. It's been cold. *Really* cold! Half of the men are sick . . ."

"Well, that's what you remember, is it?" the Narrator sighed. "If that's what you've learned, Henry, maybe you really don't want to be a Tale Traveler."

"It's just that it's been so hard. Since the storm, it's been one long, cold, wet misery. My own men don't even believe in me anymore."

"Is that all?"

"That's a lot," Henry said.

"Well then. I guess we'd better finish this chapter, don't you think?" she asked him.

"I'm ready," Henry replied.

"See you on shore!" Hope said, and she climbed onto the edge and jumped straight up into the air. Before she began to fall, she transformed again into a white gull with big childlike green eyes, and the scene began to come to life.

The high-pitched whistling of the bird was heard again.

"What's that?" Henry heard from Juan behind him.

The screech sounded again, and the young man looked up.

"It's a bird!" Juan shouted. "A bird! A bird! Land is near!" He ran back and forth on the deck of the ship gathering the crew and pointing overhead. Rodrigo rode a rope down the mast and stood with Juan staring at the sky.

"A bird! Look!" Juan continued to cheer. There wasn't just one bird now, nearly a flock of them had joined Hope, and Henry could no longer tell if she was even up there.

"Rodrigo." Juan nudged. "Rodrigo, get up there!" Rodrigo scampered back up to his post in the crow's nest on the *Santa Maria*. "Rodrigo, go! Go! Tell us what you see!" the young boy shouted excitedly.

The men cheered and pointed and cried for joy. They weren't going to fall off the world. They weren't going to have to turn around. They weren't going to die at sea. They weren't going to fail. They were going to land—in the New World.

The sky was filled with the sounds of birds and the water grew choppy, which were signs that land was near. It was almost dark for the night. The men stayed up late dancing, singing, and telling stories of the journey they had just experienced. Many of the men were cheerful about the things that once scared them. Rodrigo never left his post, even though it would have been impossible to see anything in the darkness. Juan kept checking on him and reporting back to the rest of the crew.

The stories the men shared grew from retelling what had happened into great tales of heroics. Henry was invited to join the men on the deck while they had a small stove fire and happily cooked fish knowing that it wouldn't be the only thing they would have to eat for the rest of their lives. Together they laughed and hugged and, just like the first nights of the journey, shared dreams about what they would do on land and how they would spend their riches. That night, they all felt like champion mariners and great friends.

There was no sleeping for Henry. The sky was clear once again, and he stood at the bow of the *Santa Maria* and closed his eyes while he breathed the thick sea air. Just before dawn, Henry began to notice new scents in the air. He wasn't sure that his nose could even recollect, but he thought it might be trees. Henry glanced up at Rodrigo, who still anxiously stood lookout, peeling his tired eyes across the dark water for some small hint of the landmass ahead.

The sun began to rise at their backs, and the whole ocean reflected the colors of the sunrise. Henry felt like he was floating in a giant pool of light. The surface was glassy and bright. He walked to the stern and saw the *Pinta* and the *Niña* in the distance. Against the orange glow of the ocean surface reflecting the sunrise, the two ships looked like an ancient Asian painting.

He noticed small glows coming from their decks. It must have been fires. They too had been up celebrating the nearness of land. He smiled. Henry looked forward to seeing Marty and Vicente again. For two months they had been so close and at the same time they were out of reach to him. He couldn't wait to hear the stories they would have to share about what happened on their own ships. His heart skipped lightly with anticipation.

The sky was growing brighter. Henry's crew was starting to wake. They were all happy and full of energy for the day ahead.

"Do you smell that?" Juan asked him.

"What?" said Henry.

"Trees. I smell trees," he replied. Henry must have been right. He looked at his young crewmate. Today, Henry didn't think Juan looked like a little boy. Today, he looked like a man, a sailor, a hero, and a friend.

Henry watched Juan scurry over to the mast and clamber up to the very top with Rodrigo. The entire rest of the crew had made their way to the bow and was peering into the distance with Henry. His heart was beating quickly. The sun might have been playing tricks on his eyes, but he thought he saw waves breaking ahead. There was no storm, so the white foam on the surface of the sea could only mean that the waves were striking against something. Could it really be land? Henry was breathing hard and squinting his eyes tightly to see as far as possible.

"Tierra! Tierra!" Rodrigo suddenly cried from above. His voice rang triumphantly down to his crewmates.

The call was like music in the ears of Henry and the *Santa Maria* crew.

"LAND HO! LAND HO! LAND HO," shouted Juan. He and Rodrigo jumped excitedly in the crow's nest and hugged.

Rodrigo and Juan had spotted what they all had hoped to see; and slowly, one by one, the men on deck began to believe in what their eyes were telling them. They were going to come ashore today.

Henry ran to the mast and climbed to the top with Juan and Rodrigo. Together they all waved a large flag of Spain to the *Pinta* and the *Niña* in the distance. "TIERRA! TIERRA," they shouted again and again until the other two ships also raised flags and waved them back and forth to say that they saw it too.

Henry could never remember being so excited in all his life. It took many hours from the time land was spotted to the time they were able to get to it, and he and his crew were very impatient. Many paced back and forth with nervous energy. Sometimes, the wind would change just a little and they would have to readjust the sails and it seemed to take so long when the end of the journey was so close.

Finally, at dusk, the ships had drawn as close to the shore as possible. The *Pinta* and the *Niña* were within shouting distance of the *Santa Maria*. Anchors were dropped. Strong rope ladders were unfurled from the deck at all sides.

Henry grabbed his Spanish flag and climbed down one very long ladder to the water below. The climb seemed to take ages. Then he stepped into the cool water which was up past his chest. It was hard to stand even on the tips of his toes. He waited a moment before stepping forward. When at last he had his balance, he began to wade heavily toward the beach ahead. He held up the flag so as not to put it into the water.

Henry had moved several yards from the bow of the *Santa Maria* when his men began to file in behind him. Marty had climbed off of his ship into a small side boat and was leading his crew ahead to shore. Vicente followed last with his crew right behind. Henry felt as though he was part of a long parade of great heroes marching for a crowd that would cheer for them all for hundreds of years.

The water level inched lower, from his chest to his waist, from his waist to his knees, from his knees to his ankles. At last, Henry pulled his heavy wet foot from the water and planted five tired toes solidly in the white sand of San Salvador. He pulled out his other foot and stood on the beach. It took him a moment to balance his wobbly legs on the stationary beach after having two months of rolling water beneath him.

When at last Henry turned around, he saw the hardworking men that he had come to respect and love marching toward the shore to join him, their captain. He was so proud. Soon the men were gathered around him on the quiet beach of the island of the New World. Many kissed the sandy beach and fell with joyful exhaustion to their knees or backs.

Henry held the flag high in the air for all of the men to see. "I claim the land of these Indies," he shouted above them all, "in the name of King Ferdinand and Queen Isabella, for the great country of Spain!" The men all shouted and cheered as Henry planted the flag into the ground. They had made it.

CHAPTER 10

Farewell Feast

FOR DAYS AND days they celebrated. The men drank and danced and feasted on fruit and birds. They ate *no fish*! Henry met with Marty and Vicente, and they shared tales of the amazing things each of them had gone through on their ships. They stayed warm by huge fires they built on the beaches of San Salvador.

As Henry lay one night by the side of the blazing bonfire, the smoke began to rise above him and formed the shape of a book. Henry smiled.

"Hope," he said.

The scene froze, and a spark jumped out of the fire and landed next to Henry. The spark then erupted into a huge orange flame with two green sparks at the top, and it burned quickly out leaving the green-eyed Hope in its place.

"Oh! I got singed a bit that time!" the Narrator said as she patted out a small flame on her shoulder. "Sorry about that." Then she looked down at Henry with admiration. "You made it, Henry."

"I know," he said. "I had to. I couldn't change history, you know."

"You're not looking as upset as I remember from our last visit. Do you still only remember the bad things?" she asked.

"No, Hope. I remember Bart. I remember Marty and Vicente. I remember Juan and Rodrigo and my crew. I remember getting through a storm even though we were scared to death. I remember having to eat fish and weeds for two months and how that was so awful, but it made the fruit and meat we had here taste better than any I'd ever had in my life. I remember feeling like shouting for joy when I planted that Spanish flag—"

Hope cut Henry off with a grin and a wave of her hand. "That's more like it for Christopher Columbus, but how does Henry feel?"

"Amazing!" he exclaimed. "It was the greatest adventure ever! Awesome!"

"You have many more ahead if you want to remain a Tale Traveler," she said.

"Oh, I do! But . . ." Henry stopped and sat up.

"But what?"

Henry was looking at the *Santa Maria*. In the moonlight and with the warm amber glow of the fire, she didn't look as beaten up as she really was. He couldn't see the tear down her center sail which was patchily mended with his old red velvet robes. He couldn't see the chips in the painted shields. He couldn't see the spots and dents and salt-washed wood. Tonight, the *Santa Maria* looked beautiful. She looked like home.

"Oh," said Hope as she noticed where he was looking. "You don't want to leave, do you?"

"No. I mean, I do want to do other things, and I do miss my family, and I do want to finish the book . . . the *whole* history book. But I'll miss what happens next," Henry said.

"You can't miss it," Hope kindly told him. "It already happened. This was just a small chapter of this adventure that *History* has shared with you . . . *Henry's History*."

"What did happen next though? What about Christopher Columbus? What about Bart? What about the *Santa Maria*?" Henry asked last. "She was our home."

"Soon she'll be a home to many. Look." Hope pointed to the large smoke book over them, and the pages of it began to turn. Words began to appear on them, and Hope read aloud to Henry.

"Christopher Columbus and his loyal crew discovered many other islands in the area; and on Christmas Eve, 1492, the *Santa Maria* ran aground on the north shore of Hispaniola."

"What does 'ran aground' mean?" he questioned her.

"Its bottom broke on the floor of the ocean when it came too close to shore," she told him and then continued to read. "Columbus returned to Spain on the *Niña* and left behind a group of men to settle the island. The men broke down the *Santa Maria* to build their homes. Columbus would return to the New World three more times in his life, once with Bart who was put in charge of Hispaniola. King Ferdinand would appoint Christopher Columbus admiral of the sea, just as Doña Filipa had hoped. Strangely, perhaps sadly, Christopher Columbus never even realized that he had landed in the New World but always believed that it had been the Indies."

Henry took in these words with a sort of bittersweet feeling. He was able to enjoy the journey of Christopher Columbus because he knew what it meant to history. Yet the real man who led the Enterprise of the Indies never fully appreciated the amazing thing he had accomplished. Columbus wasn't the first explorer to the Western world nor was he the last, but he was one of the most significant in history. Henry sighed deeply and smiled in spite of his sadness at leaving. Now, thanks to tale traveling, *he* got to be a part of one of those most significant moments in history too.

"Henry," said Hope, "stand up please." Hope stood first and then reached her long-fingered hand down to Henry. When he grabbed it, it felt no different than Fay's hand. Henry thought it was strange that Hope's skin should be so soft. Maybe he was just missing his little sisters.

He stood up and felt himself lifting out of his own body. Where he had been lying was a man dressed in the clothes Henry had been wearing, and he was back in his jeans and T-shirt. The scene came back to life.

"Captain," said a man coming in Henry's direction.

Henry began to answer, but the man then walked right through him. He and Hope were invisible to them all. The man went to the person lying where Henry was.

"Chris," said the man. It was Marty, and the man he was speaking to must be the real Christopher Columbus. Henry was no longer playing that role.

He looked at the island, the crews, and the captains and at the *Santa Maria*. *What a great adventure,* he thought.

"It's time," said Hope.

The two of them stood below the book of smoke, and it began to close, sucking them into the pages as it did so. Once again Henry was spinning and spinning. He saw words flashing before him again, and once again he closed his eyes until he landed with a thud.

"You all right?" asked a girl's voice.

"Yeah. I'm okay," Henry replied.

"Hey, that's pretty," said the girl. "Where did you get it?"

Henry looked down and saw that he was still wearing his chain with the *A* charm on it. He smiled.

"My wife," he said.

"Oh, very funny," said the girl.

"Why?" asked Henry.

"Well, you can't very well have a wife when you're a girl now, can you?" she answered him.

"A girl!" Henry exclaimed. He looked down at his clothes. "Not another dress," he sighed. "Here we go again."

Dear Reader,

I hope you enjoyed reading the first book in The Tale Travelers series as much as I enjoyed writing it! I've always loved reading for captive young audiences, and to share the stories that have lived in my own imagination is a dream come true. I have so many exciting adventures in store for you in this series—twenty-six of them to be exact. You'll learn more about Fay, Patty, Michael, Henry, and a young boy named Sam. Together, they will walk you through amazing adventures of true history and supernatural stories; there will be great moments in history from Henry, stunning studies in science with Sam, myths and fairy tales from many different cultures with Michael and Fay, and, with Patty, you will learn about the true and the sometimes "tall-taled" beginnings of the United States of America. Not all of the stories will be American. Tale Traveling will take you to the far ends of the earth and the far reaches of time while the five children see the world through the eyes of unfamiliar reflections and their two guides (yes, *two*!) lead them to the final chapters of their books. Getting through the story will not always be as easy as it was for Henry. What?! Did I say *easy*?! Well, it's true. The obstacles and characters The Tale Travelers will run into are great and varied and sure to keep you wondering how it will all turn out at the end of the series. Well, I can't share all of my secrets and surprises, but I assure you that your fun has just begun. One last secret that I will share is that I have no greater joy than being your storyteller. I hope you will enjoy Tale Traveling with me and enjoy the journey you take when you open any book, for they are the gifts of the storytellers of the world to the children who read them.

Sincerely,
Reji Laberje
Your Honored Storyteller

A teaser from *The Tale Travelers Book 2: Fay's Fairy Tales*

Just as quickly as the scene around Fay had frozen, it came to life again. The wind was in her hair, and she clung tightly once more to the mane of the horse. She felt the pain in her body as she bounced hard on the back of the racing animal.

"I'm coming around front!" said the third man racing beside her.

"You get him!" cried out the two men that Fay thought must be Will and Little John from when she heard those names called earlier.

Fay was scared as her horse sped faster and faster. She hoped her eyes were playing tricks on her because she looked ahead now and saw a cliff! It was a high rocky drop at the end of the wooded forest, and she was headed right toward it!

"I'm almost there, Maken!" shouted the man who was now beginning to edge in front of Fay. "Hang on! No good person shall die on my watch!"

Fay squeezed her eyes shut and held her breath. Her heart was beating so quickly that she thought it would pound right out of her chest.

Then when the edge of the cliff was just yards away . . . feet away . . . inches away . . .

To find out what happens to Fay, make sure to read *The Tale Travelers Book 2: Fay's Fairy Tales*. Also, be sure to check out www.rejilaberje.com for activities and for more updates on your favorite new series in chapter book adventures.

Guide for Teachers

(and young "tale travelers" who want to journey further)

I am always updating my Web site (www.rejilaberje.com) with information and fun reproducible activities you can implement to use The Tale Travelers and other stories in your classrooms. Drop by my Web site to request a *free* follow-up packet to *Henry's History* that includes a crossword puzzle covering the real history, a hidden clue word find that hints at Henry's next adventure while wrapping up his first, a diagram to label the learned parts of the *Santa Maria*, a maze, a reproducible sheet of bookmarks, a board game you can use in your classroom or home and—as you'll see here—a glossary and the real story of Christopher Columbus. You can also inquire about an audio copy of *Henry's History* for your school when these become available. In addition to activities and games, you will find classroom discussion topics, further recommended reading, and a description of my school visit program, an *interactive* presentation geared toward keeping children interested and, more importantly, *excited* about reading, writing, and learning. I am eager to hear any questions or comments you wish to share!

As a teacher, you have your young students' best educational interests at heart. As a children's author, I share your passion. I am overjoyed when I watch children eager to learn through reading.

What follows in the next few pages are just some of the tie-ins to the story your students have just read, and I hope it will encourage all of you to see Tale Traveling through to its conclusion. Maybe you'll also be inspired to check out my other chapter books and some of my works geared toward a younger audience. Most of all, I just hope we can team up to keep kids picking up the next book and the next one and the next one and the next one after that. I continue to be proud and honored to be your storyteller!

A SHORT GLOSSARY OF TERMS FROM
HENRY'S HISTORY

Admiral—The commander of a naval fleet.

Admiration—A feeling of pleasure, wonder, and approval

Ally—A partner, friend, or one in a helpful association with another.

Anticipation—Expectation, the act of waiting hopefully or optimistically for something.

Anxiously—Eagerly or earnestly desirous.

Bittersweet—Producing or expressing a mixture of pleasure and pain at the same time.

Bow—The front section of a ship or boat.

Card catalog—An alphabetical, organized listing (on cards or computer) of books in a library.

Chart makers—Map makers, particularly maps regarding the stars in the night skies and the seas.

Complexion—The natural color, texture, and appearance of the skin, especially the face.

Confident—Very bold, presumptuous.

Conquered—To defeat somebody by force.

Crow's nest—A basketlike platform placed high in the air in order to keep lookout for a ship.

Declared—To state emphatically or authoritatively.

Deliberate—Unmoved in action, movement, or manner as if trying to avoid error.

Doña—Spanish word meaning "Madam" or "Mrs." It is a title showing respect for women.

Editing—To correct, revise, modify, adapt, or change.

Enlisted—Engage the support or cooperation of another.

Exhausted—To be tired or worn out completely.

Grimaced—Frowned; a sharp contortion of the face to indicate pain, disgust, or dislike.

Mariners—Those who navigate or assist in navigating a ship.

Maritime—Of, relating to, or adjacent to the sea.

Mast—A tall vertical pole rising from the deck of a ship to support the sails and rigging (ropes).

Mending—Fixing by way of sewing.

Navigator—One who directs the course of a vessel.

Neglected—Something that has been failed to be cared for properly.

Objected—To express disapproval of something.

Parchment—Paper made for written text or drawing.

Pedestrians—A person traveling by foot, a walker.

Pelting—To strike repeatedly in a sharp or harsh fashion.

Port—The left-hand side of a ship when facing forward.

Quarters—A place of residence.

Scurried—To scamper; to hurry with light steps.

Señor—Spanish word meaning "Mister."

Sensation—An indefinite, generalized body feeling.

Sincerely—Genuinely and true.

Singed—To burn superficially or lightly.

Starboard—The right-hand side of a ship when facing forward.

Stern—The rear part of a ship or boat.

Suspended—To hang so as to allow free movement.

Suspicion—The act of thinking something is wrong with little evidence or proof.

Tierra—Spanish word meaning "land."

Unkempt—Not combed or properly maintained.

The Real Story of Christopher Columbus

Although remembered as something of a hero, the real life of Christopher Columbus had sad, tragic, and disappointing landmarks and endings. He was not the first explorer to the New World, nor was he the last. He was, however, one of the most historically significant as he marked the beginning of continuous European efforts to colonize the Americas. Sadly, during the 1980s and 1990s, many began to question the hero image of Columbus and instead focused on some of the more brutal aspects of European colonization and the belief that Columbus's colonies were the beginning of the destruction of Native American peoples and cultures. Regardless of this opinion, none can deny that without Christopher Columbus' mark on the world, some of today's strongest and freest societies may not exist at all. For this, in my mind, he is still a hero.

Christopher Columbus was born in 1451 in Genoa, Italy. He spent his early years learning his father's trade of weaving but later became a sailor on the Mediterranean.

In 1476, he made his way to Lisbon to join his younger brother, Bartholomew, an expert chart maker. (Following his life, Columbus would be remembered as the greatest chart maker of all time.)

In 1479 he married the well-born Doña Filipa Perestrello e Moniz.

By the age of thirty-one or thirty-two, Columbus had become a master mariner in the Portuguese merchant service. Although Columbus was not alone in the belief that one could reach land by sailing west, he was the most persistent in getting money to back his mission. He was first turned down by John II of Portugal and then at the court of Ferdinand and Isabella of Spain. Columbus came before them repeatedly for eight years before they finally said yes (as much out of exhaustion over hearing him as due to their belief in his mission).

On August 3, 1492, Columbus sailed from Palos, Spain, as captain of the *Santa Maria*. With him were the *Pinta* under Martin Alonso Pinzon and the *Niña* under Vicente Yañez Pinzon. The three ships halted at the Canary Islands, then sailed due west from September 6 until October 7, when Columbus changed course to the southwest. On October 10, a small mutiny was quelled and on October 12 he landed on San Salvador. He also discovered Cuba on October 27 and Hispaniola on December 5. After the *Santa Maria* was wrecked on Hispaniola on Christmas Eve, Henry returned to Spain on the *Niña*. He was well-received and was made "admiral of the ocean sea" and governor-general of all new lands he had discovered or should discover.

In October of 1493, he returned to the west with seventeen ships and one thousand five hundred colonists. This time, he found the Leeward Islands and Puerto Rico. The Hispaniola colony had been destroyed by natives. A new colony was created. He then found Jamaica. When he returned, he found the colonists at Hispaniola interested only in finding gold rather than creating a productive colony; he left his brother Bartholomew in charge. In 1496, he returned to Spain.

The third expedition was a sad one for Columbus. Due to the reputation of Hispaniola and the "novelty" of the New World wearing off, he was forced against his better judgment to transport convicts as colonists. On this voyage, he found Trinidad and realized (upon spotting present-day Venezuela) that he saw a whole continent. Due to the declining conditions on Hispaniola, he went against his adventurous spirit and left the continent unexplored in order to return to govern his colony (unsuccessfully). In 1500, a new governor for Hispaniola was sent by King Ferdinand and Queen Isabella, and he sent Columbus back to Spain . . . in chains.

Although Columbus was released upon his return, he was no longer popular among the native Spaniards. While his own colonies were suffering, other navigators, including Amerigo Vespucci, had been in the New World and established much of the South American coastline.

It wasn't until 1502 that Columbus had finally gathered a mere four ships to return once again to the New World in order to attempt to restore his reputation. He was still hoping to find lands answering to the description of Asia or Japan. He struck the coast of Honduras and coasted southward on the rough shoreline. He eventually reached the Gulf of Darien. He attempted to return to Hispaniola only to have to be rescued from Jamaica. He was forced to abandon his hopes one last time and return to Spain.

Columbus died less than four years later in 1506. He was mostly forgotten among the Spanish natives and was forced to go many times before King Ferdinand and Queen Isabella to beg for the money and titles he was promised after his first expedition in 1492. He claimed none of it. What's more is that, upon his death, he still believed that the lands he found were mere islands off the coast of Asia. Had his colonists been productive citizens, he may have had the luxury of exploring the continent he once spotted (South America), and only then would he have known the grandeur of the discovery he had made.

No authentic contemporary portrait of Columbus has been found. This portrait of Christopher Columbus, in the Sala de los Almirantes, Royal Alcazar, Seville, was painted by Alejo Fernández between 1505 and 1536. It is the only state-sponsored portrait of the first admiral of the Indies. Photo by Columbus Historian Manuel Rosa

BIBLIOGRAPHY

Yahoo Education/Columbia University Press. (2003) The Columbia Encyclopedia (Sixth Edition), [Website]. Available: http://education.yahoo.com/reference/encyclopedia/entry/ColumbusC [April 26, 2006]. Cohen, J.M. *The Four Voyages of Christopher Columbus,* London: Penguin Books,1969. Morison, Samuel Eliot. *The Great Explorers The European Discovery of America,* New York: Oxford University Press, 1978. Bradford, Ernle Dusgate Selby. *Christopher Columbus,* New York: Viking Press, 1973.

Koning, Hans and Bigalow, Bill. *Columbus: His Enterprise: Exploding the Myth* United States: Monthly Review Press, 1982. Fernández-Armesto, Felipe. *Columbus* New York: Oxford University Press, 1992. Axtell, James. *Beyond 1492: Encounters in Colonial America* New York: Oxford University Press, 1992. Philips, William.D. and Carla Rahn. *The Worlds of Christopher Columbus* United States: Cambridge University Press, 1992.

Reji, a proud Air Force veteran, lives near D.C. with her husband, three children, and two dogs near a network of blessed friendships. Her family is happily busy with extra curricular involvements and active in the community. Reji and her husband give their time almost exclusively to their children and their activities. She also loves music, movies, crafts, charity races and decorating. She's close with family in Wisconsin, Maine, Ohio, New York State and friends across the nation and world. Reji's favorite thing to do is read to the classrooms of her children. Learn more about the author at www. rejilaberje.com.

ABOUT THE ILLUSTRATOR . . .

Donald Ely is an illustrator & graphic designer from La Plata, MD. He graduated from the Maryland Institute College of Art in Baltimore where he received his BFA in Illustration. Clients include: Baltimore City Paper, Baltimore Magazine, Center Stage, national magazine publications and many more. Currently Donald works as the Production Assistant/Assistant Art Director at the Baltimore City Paper. He continues to illustrate in the meantime, doing freelance work and children's book illustrations. Donald likes to attend concerts in Baltimore and D.C. with his fiancée, illustrations in hand, hoping to work with his favorite musicians. Learn more at www.donaldely.com.

CD set available
(Recorded Books)